THE BITTER GREEN OF THE WILLOW

She saw a procession of white horses and scarlet outriders.

The Bitter Green of the Willow

Four Fairy Tales by March Cost *Peggy Morrison*

Illustrated by Anne Anderson

❧ Chilton Book Company

Philadelphia   New York   London

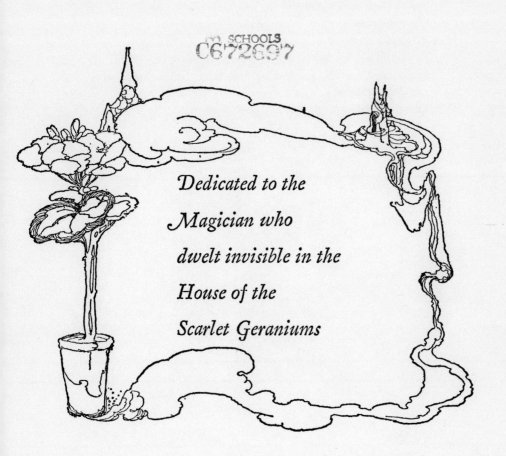

Dedicated to the
Magician who
dwelt invisible in the
House of the
Scarlet Geraniums

Contents

THE BITTER GREEN OF THE WILLOW

For the bitter green of the willow is proof against all disenchantment, as it is the only color that has reached us down the ages still dim with the tears of God.

The Strange Ship

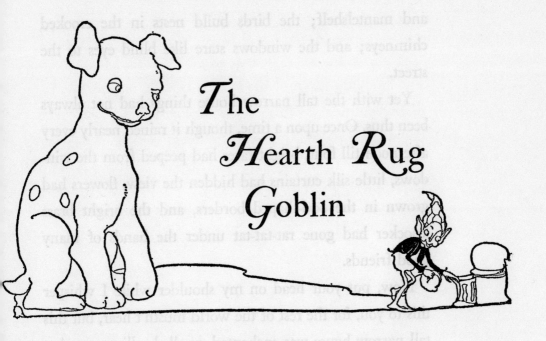

The Hearth Rug Goblin

ON the outskirts of a busy town, where it rains nearly every afternoon till four, there stands a tall narrow house, screened by four drooping willows. The gray street where it stands was once upon a time quite a busy place, but of late years people have drawn away from it farther into the town. And the large gray houses there have moss on their rhonepipes, and moss on their steps, and a half-forgotten look.

But the most lost of all is the tall narrow house I mention, for nobody lives in it any more. The plaster hangs from the walls in places; the mice hold revels on stairway and mantelshelf; the birds build nests in the crooked chimneys; and the windows stare like blind eyes to the street.

Yet with the tall narrow house things had not always been thus. Once upon a time, though it rained nearly every afternoon till four, bright faces had peeped from the windows, little silk curtains had hidden the view, flowers had grown in the odd-shaped borders, and the bright brass knocker had gone rat-tat-tat under the hands of many good friends.

Now, put your head on my shoulder while I whisper this to you, for the rest of the world mustn't hear, but this tall narrow house was enchanted, as all dwellings are that have even once had a fire lit within them, for surely you must remember from when you were very little that the very first flame that curls up the chimney gives birth to the Hearth Rug Goblin.

Now, the magic room in this tall narrow house was the room called the morning room. It had the brightest hearth in the house, for there it was that the Dear and the Dearest first smiled to each other over their breakfast cups—so, there it was the Goblin was born.

He was the size of a hazel nut, with a little round face and pointed ears, and tiny scarlet slippers. He was the busiest thing in the world, for he took all his duties closely to heart, and a Hearth Rug Goblin's life is a full one. He must spend his whole little strength, you know, making the dull things bright for us, and the bright things brighter still. And this particular little fellow was the busiest of any I ever have known.

He polished the brass ornaments till they shone like gold, he rubbed the bright fender till it dazzled the eye, he smiled on the breakfast cups and the silver tea tray till his little face nearly cracked, and the china from sheer politeness had to reflect his mirth. He danced so merrily up and down on the dark blue tiles that the China Dog with the one green eye winked slyly back to see him cut such a figure of fun. He toasted the muffins for afternoon tea the most beautiful shade of pale brown, and never once did he burn them.

Then, when the autumn days had frosted the beech leaves deep copper and gold, he helped the Fair Haired Woman at night to warm the Dark Man's slippers; and when she had nearly poked him out in her effort to make him dance extra brightly just before six o'clock, the Goblin, grinning from ear to ear, saved his life a hundred times and more by sliding down the poker till he nearly fainted from breathlessness!

Then, in the afterglow, a little after six, the man, whose name the Goblin knew was Dear, would open the door and gently kiss the cheek of the woman whose name was Dearest, as she poured out tea for him in an eggshell cup and saucer. And the canary, aslant in the sun's last ray, would twitter with mad excitement, as the Goblin turned his most showy somersault over the fender, and over the hearth rug, and danced at the woman's feet.

Now, both the Dear and Dearest were under the grown-up spell, which, after a certain age, you know, blots out all goblins, fairies, and sprites, and leaves only room for the sensible things in life, like motor buses and overcoats, toast racks and easy chairs; so neither guessed for a moment that their tall narrow house was enchanted.

Yet sometimes at dusk the woman would say, "In all the world, I don't believe there's a hearth so bright as ours," and the man would answer as he knocked out his pipe, "Yes, that chimney certainly draws very well." And the little round Goblin would wink back a tear. Could nobody see it was he?

Then one fine day, when he had almost given up hope of any one noticing him, his pointed ears heard a funny sound, and his little round eyes saw a funnier sight, for there on the hearth rug, all wrapped up, somebody blinked at him—a tiny, small creature, with chubby cheeks and little waving feet.

This little thing could not speak a word. It could only gurgle and crow, and though often the Dear and the Dearest called to it, "Darling!" it never answered them once, but winked to the Goblin Man instead, as if to say, "We'll keep them waiting, you and I," then blew the softest, most beautiful bubbles into the Goblin's cave.

This odd little thing with the waving feet had its odd little loves and hates. He loved the Goblin more each day, but he did not care for the China Dog, who sat so stiff and coldly upon the dark blue tiles. And one gloomy day, with a little wet forefinger, the Darling tried to pick out his beautiful one green eye; so after that, you understand, things were never quite the same between them, for the China Dog made it quite, quite plain this was one of those things that must never happen twice. . . .

These were the happiest days in the whole of the Goblin's life—but happy days are always short: it is the only sad thing about them, as you must have heard, you must have found since the days when you were little. One day through some sad, some sorry magic, the Darling vanished, and the Goblin's face grew dim, for he found he had no one on earth to laugh to, and nobody now to blow beautiful bubbles into his red-hot cave.

The Dear and the Dearest steadily grew more blind to him than ever, so utterly were they changed. Their faces were long, and their mouths turned down, and the Dearest entirely forgot to tie a fresh bow on the canary's cage, though he twittered and twittered that he was almost ashamed to have to sing under such a poor shabby thing.

And in those days, towards evening, the Dearest never peeped out of the window in her flowered muslin dress. She stared hard into the wall instead, and sometimes her eyes were so heavy with tears that she never noticed the Dark Man's slippers were out of the Goblin's reach. When nighttime came and the Dear returned and gently kissed her cheek, she never smiled or laughed at him, which the Goblin thought a pity, for before she had always done it so brightly; and the Goblin's hobby, you know, was bright things, as sad things made him pale. . . .

Then, as the months went by, though he still leaped merrily, madly through the bars to cheer them, he almost forgot what the man's face was like, for it never looked into the hearth with the woman's now. Instead, it wore

always a newspaper before it at breakfast, and another
before it at night.

Yet faithfully still the Goblin gleamed on the brasses,
he smiled on the china, he polished the floor, and slowly
two summers passed thus. The Dearest's dresses were no
longer of muslin, but rustled and whispered of silk, and
when she held up her two thin hands they were heavy
with sparkling stones. But, in spite of all this prettiness,
to the Goblin's surprise the Dearest never once smiled.

Then one night, when autumn had come again, and the
curtains of peacock blue shut the cold outside the windows,
the Goblin for her pleasure spun a golden web out of
scarlet flames, and paved the hearth with amber. But she
only drooped her head, and her slow tears fell through her
gleaming fingers on to the dark blue tiles.

Then at last the Goblin shuddered back. He shrank and
dwindled low, for you must have heard, you must have
known since the days when you were little, that slow,
steady tears are certain death to the poor little Goblin Man.

"This is terrible, terrible!" said the Goblin, as he drew
away from her shadow; "I shall have to take to news-
papers. . . . Yes, it has come to that."

And not till the man held his paper close against the

bars, and hid the sight of their two sad faces did the Goblin get better. As he did so, he heard the man murmur, "Only three days more to wait. . . . I always told you this house was damp."

"What shall we do with the China Dog?" said the woman dreamily; "It has lost one ear, do you see?"

"The housemaid's mother can have it," answered the man, with a laugh, "as she smashed the one you mention." And he rose and put out the lamp.

After the Dear and the Dearest left the room a hush lay over it. In the warm and shadowy quiet, only the

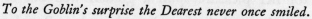

To the Goblin's surprise the Dearest never once smiled.

Grandfather Clock spoke. "You see, you see," said he fuss-ily, with the wisdom of ripe old age, "nothing is certain, nothing is sure except the time I keep."

But nobody answered him. The Goblin dared hardly glance at the China Dog lest he showed that he saw his shame. The housemaid's mother! What a truly terrible fate, and he knew how proud his yellow friend had always been of his social standing; nothing less than the best Dutch tiles had ever supported him. With downcast eyes, in the shadowy fireplace the Goblin moved towards him.

"You heard what he said?" said the China Dog hoarsely. "After years of service, this is what happens to me. The housemaid's mother, forsooth! Why, she hasn't a tile to her grate—she has only a kitchen range! Now I will prob-ably spend my last days on a vulgar crocheted mat, perched on some showy shelf!" And he shuddered through and through.

"I'm *sorry*," answered the Goblin, "but it may not be as bad as you think, though I can't imagine why they're doing this when every one knows you've always been such an addition to the grate."

"Why!" cried the China Dog, "haven't you seen, haven't you heard? Don't you understand? They're going away themselves, and *you'll* have to go out for good at last."

"Going away!" cried the Goblin, his heart dropping into his little red shoes. "Oh, surely not. You have made a mistake . . . for what would become of me?"

"*I'm* sorry for *you*," said the China Dog, "for yours is truly a black outlook. And although I never cared for your flighty ways, still you have my sympathy, for we've always got on very well together, as I'm nothing if not broadminded. But you see *at last* what a fool you've been to keep things bright for them when they never noticed at all."

"What will become of me now?" the Goblin whispered, with fear, to himself.

"Cheer up!" said the China Dog. "It is a bit of a wrench, but you ought to be glad. Your busy, polishing days are done. Haven't you got your release at last? The last time your fire is lit, you have only to mount to the sky on your final smoke wreath, and in that most comfortable moon hotel spend your afterlife in idleness, with the stars to keep things bright for you entirely free of charge."

"Oh! yes, quite so, quite so!" said the Goblin, smiling a wan little smile across the darkening room, his round eyes still dazed with shock.

"But you must take care," the China Dog continued, his tone much warmer now that he was dealing with advice, "that you do not miss your last smoke wreath, for then you will have to wait till the fire is lit again—and goodness knows when *that* will be. No one will buy this house in a hurry. It is certainly far too damp."

The Goblin made no answer.

"You hear me?" said the China Dog, "I'm only warning you, for you *know* you have such a habit of dawdling, lingering over last touches when there's nobody there to see."

Still the Goblin made no answer. His voice was lost in huskiness, and he had no breath to spare. His biggest moment had caught him as it catches many just when their light is lowest, and he was fighting for his very life. Two great tears had suddenly swum into his round, black eyes, and he knew he dare not let them fall on the points of his scarlet slippers—for you must have heard, you must have known since the days when you were little, that slow, steady tears are certain death to the poor little Goblin Man.

The Yellow Dog gave a short, sharp snort, and turned him his coldest shoulder. Then, as the embers flickered low, he puffily fell asleep and forgot such sorrows as crocheted mats in a dream world full of best tiled hearths, where housemaids' mothers have no entry, and kitchen ranges are never mentioned.

In the silence the Grandfather Clock spoke once, then twice, then thrice, for his was always the final word, and he liked this advertised even when there were no replies. But though he stayed dumb as a broken bell the whole night through, the Goblin Man slept not a wink in case his two sad tears dropped out.

Next morning his fire was kindled again, and the morning after that, too, but though on the third day he leaped, he danced, he whirled, he spun as brightly, as gaily as ever, the table, the chairs, and the shining brasses were one by one taken from him before he could polish them twice. Soon nothing remained in the room but the empty walls and the floor and a cobweb on the roof. The Goblin shrank back in despair at all this loneliness, then just as his embers dwindled low, the man and the woman looked into the room together.

"I don't think we've left anything," she said. "How empty it all looks now. Why! I believe the fire is still alight."

"Yes, that chimney always drew well," said the man, with his hand on the door, "but I always told you the house was damp."

"Don't go! Don't go!" cried the Goblin at that, pulling

himself through the bars and flinging his last bright light at their feet. But neither the Dear nor the Dearest heard him, and they shut the door in his face.

A little wisp of pale blue smoke curled out and round like a broken ring, then vanished up the chimney.

"You are a little fool!" said a long-lost Sixpence from a chink in the floor. "The last smoke wreath has gone up without you. You will have to become a ghost now."

The Goblin shivered where he stood. "They will come back," he said huskily. "They will come back and light the fire."

"They will never come back," said the long-lost Sixpence. "Personally, I don't mind, for my value increases every day I lie here idle. In fact, if I stay here long enough the world may forget I am only one of the common family of Sixpence. Now that I have nothing to do with the till, I may later on be taken by the entire county, the people who really know, as a real Coyn—you never can tell!" Her voice rose shrilly from the dusty floor. "In fact, I may yet be buried in the British Museum."

Far down the stairs the front door banged for the last time.

The Goblin turned pale as ashes, from his little round

face and pointed ears to the tips of his scarlet shoes. He ran to the window, and peered through a chink in the shutter.

The Dear and the Dearest went down the path in the watery afternoon light, and never once looked back. They climbed up into a shiny black cab which rattled them out of sight under the shivering branches. Then, last of all, the housemaid's mother, in her rusty black cloak and the bonnet with feathers, hobbled towards the gate with two broken loaves and the China Dog in her basket, and the man's old office umbrella hooked over her arm.

Between the drooping willow trees the gate clanged dully after her and only woke one echo. Along the narrow, damp-edged garden path the dead leaves whispered fretfully, then lay quite still. And rain began to fall. . . .

Years have passed by since that autumn afternoon, and the house is still for sale. The plaster hangs from the walls in places; the birds build nests in the crooked chimneys; the windows stare like blind eyes to the street—and nobody wants to buy it. And those people who do chance to pass it each day with their brown kid gloves and shabby umbrellas never guess that this tall narrow house is enchanted; for nobody ever sees a round little, white little face, the size of a hazel nut, peering out from a chink in the shutter.

This story hasn't an end yet, or else I would tell you it now. Instead, I want you, oh! so badly, to do something for me if only you will. Will you save up all your pennies and buy that house for me again, and release the Goblin Man? We shall only have to light a fire in the room that faces south to be happy ever after all our lives. . . .

You will know the house at once, for it rains there nearly every afternoon till four. There are four drooping willow trees screening it from view, and a signboard flapping in the wind.

*T*he *R*ose *C*olored *S*pectacles

DO you remember when you were seven and I was six, they told us London was the hub of the universe, and we never could understand what this was, or why? At last I have found the reason, and here is this little tale for you, though when you begin to read it, you will have quite forgotten we ever wondered together about it, over a hundred years ago.

This is the story, then, of the queer Old Man and his queer old shop that stood in a queer old street, for at last I am able to tell you the reason the dusty wheel of the world turns round about London Town is simply because this old person keeps his queer old dusty shop there.

Now, in the days when we were little and only reached to the front door handle, nobody ever told us how very important the Old Man was; and somehow we never guessed, for he lived in the poorest part of the city, where the lamplight is mean and thin, and before you could reach his shop you had to pass for a long, long way through crisscross roads, playing hide-and-seek round tired old buildings with slates aslant and unsteady steps.

Then you came to a certain street that was darker and narrower than all the others, and where creaking lamps shook only a weak pool of light beneath them at every corner. In the dark hours the air of this queer old street was chill, with a smell of damp like a moss-grown well, but in the light and morning hours you could see easily enough at one end the Daytime Home for little new babies, and the Undertaker's shop at the other, and, in between, the deep set doors of the Butcher, the Baker, the Candlestick Maker, with a Cobbler or two, and the old Sweetmakers.

And I can remember (though you have forgotten) their windows made of dull glass had little knots in the leaded panes, which mixed in wheels of orange and blue and green the colors of all the wares within.

Now, the oldest shop in this queer old street was the

Curio Shop of the queer Old Man. And it was very old. In fact, the good-for-nothing Pavement Artist, who made his bread-and-butter pennies by adding fancy flourishes to the signs of other men, sometimes told the Milk Boy that the Old Man had opened his shop there before the street itself! But the Milk Boy never believed this. He just winked his eye and brought round his milk cans later than ever that day, for he knew well enough the Old Man had certainly been there from the beginning, surely a good enough start for any one, without going farther back.

And I can remember (though you have forgotten) the panes of the Old Man's deep window were extra thick and very dark, and though behind there lay rich brocades from France, fine silks from China Town, ivories from India, and sparkling glass from Venice, all you could see from the outside were those crazy little wheels of color whirling in blue and orange and green.

But there was always one little pane in the left-hand corner against which, if you pressed your nose, you could see past the wheels of color to the carven fans, the frail lace shawls, and the gay china figures within. Sometimes, too, if you pressed your nose to a shiny, white-rimmed button, you caught a glimpse of the shop beyond, but only a glimpse, for the roof was low and hung with shadows, and curtains darkened the walls.

Sometimes, if you pressed your nose, you caught a glimpse of the shop beyond.

Still, you could always manage to steal a blink of quaint figures in bronze and copper gleaming dimly down from the crowded shelves, but you were careful never to press your nose very long to the left-hand pane in the late afternoon, when the shadows thickened so slyly, for within, on a dusty pedestal, the large green idol with the twisted smile and yellow eyes would stare at you through and through, as if he had suddenly come alive in the dusk, and was hating you very silently.

Although the Old Man was tired and bent and gray, and never left the dark and crooked street, and although his face was wrinkled like sand where the sea had furrowed it, he never seemed to grow any older. And people whispered at evening when they saw him sweep out his shop, "See! He has forgotten how to die!"

After he put up his shutters at night nobody knew what he did behind them, or how his lonely evenings passed. Some said he slept like a dormouse till dawn, others that he changed to a spider at midnight, and spun his own frail shawls, for the sick person lying awake in the house across the street had often watched his light, through a chink in the shutter, burning *the whole night through.* But nobody really knew anything at all about him, except that he was a strange, a very strange old man.

Many customers came to his shop by daytime, for he

was known to have many treasures, and these they would turn over eagerly, while the Old Man, unheeding, went on with his work of mending perhaps a damaged crucifix from Rome, or maybe a broken idol from Basra.

Now, the oddest of all the Old Man's wares was a pair of Rose Colored Spectacles that lay on a black little silken cushion, but to most would-be buyers (and there were many) he always shook his head.

"They are a curiosity," he would say, "and I have a special price of my own for them. They would be useless to you. See, instead, here is an amulet from the tomb of the greatest Pharaoh, and a little jade heart that belonged to a Persian Princess."

And in the tiny, overcrowded shop where Dresden shepherdesses were coldly elbowed by slim and naked figures from Greece, where snuffboxes lay side by side with happy charms, and glossy portraits smiled bravely from dull frames—in all this jumble of valuable odds and ends, the Old Man would hold his treasures against the light, till they seemed alive with a secret life, in the dusty golden glow that the afternoon sun always left in his low-roofed place.

Then at last it happened that one day towards evening, as the Old Man stood alone in his shop, mending a golden ring from far Stamboul, he saw the Young Thing pass his window, and open the creaking door. The Old Man did not lift his head while the Young Thing fingered his wares. He went on quietly mending the ring from far Stamboul.

"You have a fine collection here," said the Young Thing pleasantly.

"A thing or two, a thing or two," said the Old Man, without looking up.

"How much are those Rose Colored Spectacles?" then asked the other. "I have never seen anything quite so pretty before."

"Ah!" and the Old Man glanced up at that, "I have a special price for these," and he lifted them very gently with his worn but nimble fingers. "I would not sell them to everyone."

"But surely to me!" said the Young Thing brightly. "I will give you a very good price for them."

"Well, well," said the Old Man, "perhaps, perhaps. . . . You are young and happy, and it is good to be that, so I'll let you have them cheap."

"Then what do they cost?" asked the Young Thing, a trifle impatiently.

The Old Man smiled. "Oh! an odd little price, an odd

little price! A charge of my own, in fact. Only this silver cup full of your bitterest tears."

"You must be mad!" laughed the Young Thing gaily, "as mad as a mad March hare. Why, I haven't a single tear to give you!"

"Come! Come!" said the Old Man, smiling still, "this is only an old man's joke. These things are given away now. I will not press my account," and he handed them over the counter.

"Well," said the Young Thing, "although you are certainly mad you are generous too, and I never forget a kindness. You have many beautiful things here. I will send you many customers."

"Well, well, we shall see," said the Old Man in his even voice, as the Young Thing turned to the door. "Take care that you do not break these glasses, though, for there are no others your size in stock."

"I always take care," said the Young Thing hastily, upsetting a small tray of bric-a-brac. "Now, that is a stupid place to put such a tray as this, just at one's very elbow. However, good day and good-bye."

The Old Man made no answer. He did not seem to hear, for he had picked up once again the broken ring from far Stamboul. A minute later he shivered slightly.

"They always leave the door open," he muttered, wearily crossing the floor, "as long as they're not behind it."

Then he put up his shutters, and closed his shop, but, before he went to his workroom, he tapped on a little barometer that hung in the shadows behind him. He tapped on it once, he tapped on it twice, and, "Rising . . . rising," he muttered. Then very bent, and very gray, and very, very old, he passed behind his workshop door, where no one has ever seen, but mice have been heard to grumble that the crumbs are made of pink glass.

And the days passed by, and the nights passed by, and the Old Man's life went on as before, though now when he tapped on his little barometer, he always muttered, "Falling . . . falling."

Then one day at dusk, while the rim of the sky was still golden, though shadows like thieves had slipped through the streets, the door of the Old Man's shop slowly opened, and the Young Thing stood before him.

The Old Man went on mending a scented phial from gay Seville.

"Old Man," said the Young Thing huskily, "I have brought back the broken bits."

The Old Man looked over his glasses. "How did it happen?" he slowly asked. "I told you to take great care."

"I *took* great care," the Young Thing said. "You know I always do—it's a thing I make a point of—but one day I lent them to a friend who dropped them underfoot. You must sell me another pair at once, for now I can hardly see without them."

"I'm sorry," said the Old Man, "but I warned you at the beginning. There are no others your size in stock."

The Young Thing stood as if turned to stone. A stillness that was thick and eerie hung in the little shop. The web of the shadows grew deeper, and the golden rim of the sky turned green. Then the Young Thing's voice, with pain, turned sharp as the bits of rose colored glass that winked in the dusty light. "At least you will mend these for me again. . . . I will pay you any price. . . . Old Man, I *cannot* do without them."

"I have a charge of my own," replied the Old Man, "an odd little price, an odd little price. Money had nothing to do with these glasses. No, not from the very beginning. Indeed you might say they were priceless—still, I am very honest, so I will tell you the truth. I cannot mend them for you. They are broken beyond repair. . . . Can you see your way to the door?"

The Young Thing staggered, then "I have gone blind," came the whisper. "How shall I manage now?"

"You must feel your way," said the Old Man. "That is the only way."

"You do not understand," said the Young Thing hoarsely. "I had a very long way to go."

"Well," said the Old Man, "perhaps you may feel your way more quickly than in the past you have seen it. . . . I have known this sometimes happen."

"You are mad," said the Young Thing brokenly, "as mad as a mad March hare. I have reached my journey's end."

"Not at all, not at all," said the weary Old Man. "You have certainly passed the Sunshine milestone, and come to the one called Shadow, but at neither of these does a journey end. Good night. You have indeed a long way to go." And he turned to his work again.

The Young Thing did not answer, but stumbled through the door. The Old Man went on mending the scented phial from gay Seville. A moment later he shivered. "They always leave the door open," he muttered, wearily crossing the floor, "as long as they are not behind it." And he gazed down the street with his long-sighted eyes to make quite sure that the Young Thing would never come back again.

Then he put up his shutters, and closed his shop, and made things safe for the night. And last of all, with his worn but nimble forefinger, he tapped on his little barometer that hung in the shadows behind him. He tapped on it once, he tapped on it twice, and then, "No change," he muttered. Then slowly he bent, and with painful care he gathered up all the winking fragments that had cost a beaker of tears.

Very wearily, but very daintily, with all delicate care, the Old Man spread on an ivory slab these little broken bits. Then he hobbled with them through the doorway of his little dark workroom. And all through the long hours of evening and the chilly hours of dawn he never once came out, but stayed within in that little room where no one has ever seen, though the mice have been heard to grumble that the crumbs are made of pink glass, that the window is screened by a shadow blacker than any night, while the walls are hung with cobwebs, and the carpet made of dust.

Then, very early on a still, moist morning, before the sun had had a chance to line the sooty chimney pots with bright, false gold, or the first frowsy sparrow waked amid a sleepy twitter-twitter—when the Covent Garden flower carts had rattled across the cobbles of the queer old street, and brushed its misty gray with little foreign scents, and sudden glows of color—just as the blue-nosed Milk Boy,

"No change!" he muttered.

ten minutes late as usual, jangled his cans outside each sleepy door, the Old Man crept from his workroom, crooked and huddled and bent. Very wearily, very daintily, with all delicate care, he laid on the black little silken cushion a pair of Rose Colored Spectacles.

Then he tapped on his little barometer with his worn but nimble finger. He tapped on it once, he tapped on it twice, and still, "No change!" he muttered.

Then, sighing a little, for he was a very tired Old Man, he opened the door, he took down his shutters, he swept out his shop, and awaited his next customer. . . .

How can I tell all this, you ask, of the queer Old Man and his queer old shop, where the window panes whirl in rainbow colors, and the afternoon sunshine sometimes leaves a pool of gold in the dusty place?

But that is another story, and you mustn't ask me twice, for it happened long after the time when I was six and you were seven, and we wondered why things were. . . .

I must keep it for that other day when things are once more topsy-turvy, and the world is very beautiful because there's cake for tea—and both of us can barely reach that shiny Front Door Handle.

The Strange Ship

WITHIN the ruined mill that lies beyond that far-off wood, there lived for many years the Old Miniature Painter, once Artist-in-Chief to the Royal Court of Vanity Fair, in the city of Hum Drum. His sight failing, he very sorrowfully one day moved there with his box of paints, his brushes, and his ivories, for he found every one refused quite definitely to buy his portraits, now that he gave them as often as not green cheeks, and cobalt lips, and large eyes of crimson lake.

Now, never having had a head for sums, he had spent his money as it came, to make things easier all round. So, when his eyesight failed, he found with something of a shock all he had left was a tiny daughter and a number of threepenny bits, which lived in a small, very red little bank.

So, with a deep sigh, his tiny daughter and the bank of threepenny bits, he made his way to the ruined mill beyond the far-off wood.

Years passed, and the child of the Old Miniature Painter, whom he called the Little Loved One, grew up with the woodcutter's children, and spent her days romping with them through the mouse-haunted barns, where cobwebs hung like torn shawls from the rafters, or fishing with them for darting minnows, where the mill waters swirl into deep green pools, under gray, drooping willows.

Then, one day, on her fifteenth birthday, she chanced to stray farther than usual through the mazy wood, and, from a clearing in the trees, she looked for the first time downhill to where the red, stained roofs of a distant town shone by a purple-blue sea. As she stared she saw upon the road below her a procession of white horses and scarlet outriders, then a gold coach followed by a gay multitude waving banners, and marching bravely to the sound of many trumpets.

Running eagerly down this hill, she peered, bright eyed,

through a bramble hedge, and was just in time to see the coach sweep round the corner, and seated within a tall person with dark brown hair and eyes, an ermine cloak, and a chain of gold. Then the next minute he was hidden by the marching multitude and the swaying flags.

With a fast-beating heart, and powdered with white road dust, she ran back through the damp, still wood, and told the Miniature Painter of what she had seen. She found him busily engaged in trying to shake out one of their few remaining threepenny bits. "Ah," he answered her, "that must be the new Lord Mayor of Hum Drum."

"Father!" she cried suddenly, and there were tears in her voice, "I long so much for the bright red roofs of that city by the sea! I am tired, so tired of this wood, with its heavy lichens, and soft fussy murmurs that really mean nothing at all. I am tired, so tired of these mouse-haunted chambers and choked by their dusty stillness. I am tired of these tattered cobwebs and the bitter green of the willow."

"Be patient, my child," said the Old Miniature Painter, "and believe me, *this* spot looks just as fair from the city of Hum Drum, for it is only the distance in between which really makes the picture. But, one day I promise you, when you are able to paint more skillfully, we will journey to Hum Drum together that you may prove this for yourself."

But, alas, in three years' time, when the Little Loved One could paint miniatures with as fairy-like a touch as the delicate tinting that trembles on a butterfly wing, the Old Miniature Painter died. And the night before this happened he took her little hands in his, and said with much earnestness, "My child, as you grow older, you will find beauty is of much greater importance than happiness, and as happiness is too small a thing to bless you with, I will pray for you all beauty."

"How strangely he speaks," whispered the Little Loved One to the woodcutter's wife, and then she ran to the cupboard, and made him a large comforting bowl of gruel. But next day he died, and his last words to her were, "Never leave your paint brushes in water, and always remember, for I, an old man, who have seen all colors, tell you that there is no color so beautiful as the bitter green of the willow."

The Little Loved One wept, but she did not sob, for his face bore the contented look of one who has passed the first stage of a difficult journey, on the whole, successfully.

Then very sorrowfully, with his box of paints, his brushes, and his ivories, she set out all alone for the city of Hum Drum.

For two days and two nights she journeyed there by foot, and on the morning of the third day, lo! when she shook out the last threepenny bit on to the roadway, to her amazement she found it was a piece of gold.

"Now," she said joyfully, "I am a wanderer no longer, for I shall buy a little house, a little furniture, and some new paint and brushes. Perhaps in a little I may even

To her amazement she found it was a piece of gold.

become famous, and perhaps the Lord Mayor may yet come to tea with me."

So she ran down the highway into the city of Hum Drum, where the winds of the sea, even on the sunniest day, whistle a warning round each corner. Then, when she reached the oldest part of the town, she suddenly stopped short, for there before her she saw a tiny crooked house with the top story overhanging the bottom one, like a heavy eyelid, with one half of its windows gazing in a shortsighted way through trees into the street, and the other half gazing with a faraway look over the cliffs to sea. And above the front door, which had five little steps and a bright brass knocker, there was a signboard with the words: "The Lonely House—To Let."

So the Little Loved One ran up the steps, and bought the little house with the gold threepenny bit, and with the change she also bought a little bed, a little table, a little chair, a little cup and saucer, a little pot, a tin of Brasso, and a few dusters. Then, carefully hanging her best miniatures in her front window, which faced the street, she settled down—and that is the first part of the story.

One week passed, and the Little Loved One worked very hard. Soon many people came to have their portraits painted, and all were charmed, as she always managed to paint every one looking just as they liked to think they looked. Then with the first money she made, she hastened out and bought another chair, and another cup and saucer, and when she unpacked them in the Lonely House, she said joyfully, "You never know! The Lord Mayor may come for tea any day now."

That night, after she had shut her little house and gone to bed, the rain lashed so hard against her window, and the wind howled so loudly down her chimney that she could not sleep. Then, as she lay there shivering, listening with a loud beating heart to the storm, she became aware, as the wind died down in gusts, of a strange sound without, of footsteps pacing steadily up and down upon the pavement.

"Who can be abroad on such a dreadful night?" she wondered; then, listening for the rise and fall of the strange footsteps, she softly fell asleep.

Next morning, when she rubbed her eyes in the sunshine, there before her in the little house, she saw *three* cups and saucers, and *three* little chairs. "How can this be?" she said, bewildered, "when I only bought and paid for two?"

But the things within the Lonely House made no reply, and the Third Cup and Saucer, and the Third Chair sat stiff and silent, but quite as real as the other two. So the Little Loved One got out her dusters and polished them as well, for she felt somehow certain the Lord Mayor would drive past her door that day, and perhaps even call and drink tea.

At a quarter to four, then, she set out her table with two little cups and saucers, and two little chairs; and at four o'clock, sure enough, there came the sound of many trum-

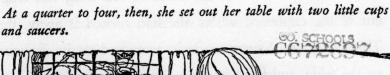

At a quarter to four, then, she set out her table with two little cups and saucers.

pets, then the flash of white and scarlet outriders, then the gold coach, and the Lord Mayor looking as handsome and as unlike a Lord Mayor as it is possible to look.

Surrounded by at least half a dozen Town Councilors, the Lord Mayor strode up the five little steps and demanded a cup of tea. When the Little Loved One, trembling with excitement, explained there weren't enough cups to go round, he left his followers on the mat, and sat down alone while she poured out tea.

Then it was that the most curious thing of all happened in the Lonely House of the Little Loved One, for, from out of the cupboard where she had tucked it away, the Third Cup and Saucer made its way, and set itself down on the table, and from its place against the wall the Third Chair walked across the room, and sat down at table with them.

"What an extraordinary thing!" said the Lord Mayor, greatly interested. "Where did you get your performing furniture?"

"I'm sure I cannot tell you," the Little Loved One replied. "It just seems to have happened in the night."

So pleased was the Lord Mayor with this entertainment that he placed an order for a miniature of each of his

Town Councilors on the spot. "You see, I have to give them something every Christmas," he said. "They expect it. And as they all have umbrellas, and I never can remember what size they take in gloves, this will save me a lot of trouble, and be more lasting, too."

But when the Little Loved One had thanked him gratefully, he suddenly sighed deeply, laid down his bread and honey, and began to tell her his secret worry, which, he said, spoiled all the joy of being Lord Mayor of Hum Drum.

With knitted brow and lowered voice, he told her then of that Strange Ship with ghostly sails, which, manned by no living hand, steals silent as a snake within the harbor of Hum Drum, and anchors there perhaps an hour, perhaps three; and then at sunset, with the turning of the tide, sets sail again, and drifts across the bar.

"Before the Ship is sighted by us," the Lord Mayor told her, "always a strange green light pours upon the town, and then the people in the cliff houses pull down their blinds and bar their doors, and the townsfolk in the streets rush home to do the same, all in the wildest flurry. Some, the bravest, who have peeped between their shutters and watched the Ship set forth again, say that when it sails away it floats upon its mast a royal purple standard, though no one here can guess who runs it up, as none has yet been sighted upon the decks."

"But—" began the Little Loved One.

"Don't interrupt," said the Lord Mayor firmly, "or else I'll lose the thread. Then when morning comes again, and I hasten to the marketplace with the Town Crier and my Councilors, we always find—" his voice became a whisper.

"Yes?" said the Little Loved One, shivering in her little shoes.

"—that one of us is missing. And never once," the Lord Mayor concluded, "has any missing soul returned."

"Oh, dear! Oh, dear!" said the Little Loved One, "I am so very sorry." And she poured out a second cup of tea for him, so that by the time the Lord Mayor finished, he felt a good deal more cheerful, and went away shaking hands, and looking handsomer than ever. On the bottom step, he called back, "I have enjoyed myself very much, and will make a point of drinking tea with you every second Thursday, and telling you my other worries."

And so he did, and every second Thursday after that became the red-letter day in the Lonely House's calendar, for by this time the Little Loved One felt quite sure he was really her happy ending. And really, when you come to think of it, everything seemed to point that way, for nowadays he always dropped the Lord Mayor's chain with a great clank upon the threshold, and one day told her that he loved her.

And at every tea party they had together the Third Cup and Saucer made its way from the cupboard, and the Third Lonely Chair joined them at the table. But, curiously enough, although he had laughed very much on the first occasion, the second time the Lord Mayor only smiled, and the third time his face did nothing, and the fourth time very faintly it frowned, while the *fifth* time it frowned harder. "I cannot understand this performance," he told her gloomily, for being Lord Mayor he liked to feel he was the only one.

So the Little Loved One, with her heart aquiver, to please him, jumped up and said, "I know what I will do to end it once and for all." And she ran to her little ribbon box, and tied the Third Chair with a piece of lavender silk to a hook in the wall, then she took up the Third Cup and Saucer, and smashed them on the hearth.

The Lord Mayor smiled again, but the Little Loved One's heart gave an odd little thump as she watched the broken primrose-colored pieces at her feet, for it was the first cruel thing she had ever done in her life.

But just then a sharp sound made her turn swiftly round, for the Lord Mayor had jumped to his feet with a sudden cry, and as she followed his eyes, she saw the Third Chair slowly untie the lavender silk and then very slowly walk to the table again. As he watched, the Lord Mayor's face grew a shade less brown, and the Little Loved One's grew pale as one of her ivories.

Then, as if spellbound, both turned towards the hearth, and there, before their very eyes, they saw the primrose pieces rise, and silently fit themselves once more into the Third Cup and Saucer, which then, very slowly but very surely, made its way to the table, and joined them once more at tea.

The Lord Mayor walked to the door with a heavy tread, and put on his gold chain again to make him feel he was real. "Good-bye," he said, "for now I am sure that you are really a witch." And he shut the door with a good hard slam.

"Come back! Come back!" cried the Little Loved One, and she ran to the door, but all she saw was the drooping trees that hid the house from the street, and all she heard was the hollow sound of coach wheels rolling farther away. "Oh, dear!" said the Little Loved One, "now he will never come back."

Yet when the next second Thursday came round, she set out her tiny tea table, and ran to the window to watch. And four o'clock came. "He is bound to be late today," she said. "I know he cannot come today before it is half past four." And when the clock in the Lonely House chimed half past four, "I could not expect him before five now," she whispered. And then when, with a little shiver, the clock on the wall chimed six, she told herself, "I will wait until seven, then I will put the tea things back in the cupboard." . . . And she put them back at eight.

Then that very night, at the hour when she leaned from her top lattice, with her eyes bent on the willow boughs which hid her house from the street, she remembered her father's words, and in the silence there, she spoke her wonder alone.

"Oh! why did he find you beautiful, willows, drooping so sadly there?" Then, with a tiny shock, she suddenly heard an unknown voice from the shadows below her reply, "For the bitter green of the willow is proof against all disenchantment, as it is the only color that has reached us down the ages still dim with the tears of God."

"Who goes there?" said the Little Loved One, in a whisper, leaning farther out from the lattice. But all she heard in the gloom was a quiet little laugh as of one amazed, then the voice replied simply, "A friend." There was a tiny pause while the leaves trembled together, then "Pass, friend, in peace," she said gently, and softly shut her lattice. And within, to herself, she said, "So I am not then quite alone. It would appear I still have two things left, the tears of God and a friend."

And the days lagged into weeks, and the weeks dragged into months—and never once did the Lord Mayor stop at her doorway, though she sometimes saw him drive past, looking as handsome as ever, and if anything just a shade less thin, for things in his city prospered, and in all that time the Strange Ship called not once.

But alone in the Lonely House things did not prosper, for now the Little Loved One gave every one she painted such a very sad expression that soon only her poorest customers, the young and the romantic, were left to her; and in a little, when her eyes grew heavier still with unshed tears, and she began, like her father before her, to give these last green cheeks and cobalt lips and large eyes of crimson lake, these also indignantly departed.

And so for a year and a day she lived thus sadly in the little forsaken house, with the three ghostly cups and saucers and the three lonely chairs, and the only footsteps she ever heard now were those unknown ones at midnight pacing to and fro below her window. Then, on the second day of the second year, which fell on a second Thursday, at four o'clock, with a flourish of trumpets, suddenly the Lord Mayor's coach stopped outside the little Lonely House.

Her heart, trembling with joy like a candle set in a windy place, the Little Loved One ran to the door and opened it, her eyes shining through like wet stars.

The Lord Mayor entered, looking as brown and as handsome as ever, but certainly not in the least bit thin. He did not drop his cloak nor his chain of gold, but he stood erect before the Loved One as if in the City Chambers, and in that clear but empty voice with which people in Parliament make speeches: "I have come to tell you," he said, "that you will have to remove from this house by the thirty-first of May."

The Little Loved One's eyes grew wide, and her heart seemed to jag within her like a rusty darning needle, but "Why?" was the only word she had strength to say.

"Official reasons," replied the Lord Mayor. "Also some of my relatives object that your roof blocks out their view in a most distressing way."

"But," said the Little Loved One, in a voice that was husky with many silences, "what shall I do? There is nowhere else I can go," and her tears fell on to his buckled shoes and left little blurs on the silver.

"Don't do that," said the Lord Mayor sharply, and drawing quickly away. "There really is no reason why you should trouble, for I am very sure your performing furniture will always stand you in good stead."

As he spoke, the room darkened a little, as if outside the sun drifted behind a cloud, and without it the trees drained only a green light through the window. The Little Loved One stared into his face, for she could hardly believe it was he who had spoken. Then he walked very quickly to the door.

"I've got rather a headache," he said, as he took his leave. "I believe there is thunder in the air."

He stretched out his hand to the handle. He opened the door, and a rush of green light poured into the room like water and lit up the things within it. Then through the open door, down that stone street, came the rush of many frightened feet, and the shouts of many frightened souls—faster, faster, flowing past the door, leaving the air full of clamor.

"What's this?" cried the Lord Mayor, starting back sternly, and the rushing voices answered him as he joined them, "The Strange Ship has crossed the bar."

"The flag I see is black!"

Then in torrents came the rain, in such force that it lashed the stoneway of Hum Drum till a mist like low, gray smoke seemed to run along the ground; and when three hours later the Ship put out to sea again, the Little Loved One's eyes were the only ones that followed it, for her little house had not a single shutter (only five little steps and a bright brass knocker).

Looking through her lattice, she whispered brokenly, "They say it floats a purple standard, and now I know that I am going blind, for the flag I see is black."

Next day at noon the Lord Mayor with his Town Councilors assembled in the marketplace, and read the roll aloud to trace the missing soul, but lo! each answered to his name.

"What is the meaning of this?" demanded the Lord Mayor, and he read the roll again, and lo! again each answered to his name. At the third reading the townsfolk all began to mutter and cast uneasy looks at one another, and each look seemed to say, "Yes, our *bodies* all are here, yet whose *soul* has gone aboard?" And each, with one exception, went home deeply troubled lest his own had died. And in the days that followed before the thirty-first of May, a curious change took place among the people of Hum Drum, for their faces lost their usual comfortable

The Lord Mayor with his Town Councilors assembled in the marketplace.

expressions. All were haunted now by an inner fear that left each face a little pale and strained.

Then, on the thirty-first of May, with scarlet outriders and coach of gold, the Lord Mayor drove proudly past the Lonely House. "How strange," he said to himself with a laugh that woke echoes under the mossy archway, "that these windows ever haunted me!" And to his Councilors he called aloud, "It is not even worth pulling down! Let that house stand till it falls."

And the coach swept round the corner of the red-roofed town where even on the sunniest days the wind shrieks warning always, but behind her spotted muslin curtains, instead of dancing with joy at the news that her Lonely House might stand, the Little Loved One shivered with dread.

In gazing at the Lord Mayor's face, so brown and so self-assured in the ring of pale, uncertain ones, she suddenly knew his was the soul the Ship had stolen. And a long-ago memory like a spell came back to her, and out of a dim chamber where cobwebs hung like torn shawls from the rafters, and the air was choked by a dusty stillness, she heard the words of the very Old Miniature Painter, that beauty is more to be valued than joy.

And again she shivered with dread when she thought of the Lord Mayor's face. "How terrible," she said, "to live with an empty joy like that which only wakes hollow echoes, to be locked up for ever in a world of cardboard things."

And she bowed her head and wept, for although her love had died, she was still troubled by pity for him. But in a little she dried her eyes, long before her mouth had ceased to tremble.

Then half fearfully she whispered to herself, "I must let him out of his cardboard kingdom, as he cannot help himself." And all day long she thought and thought how this could be done. Then at four o'clock, for the first time in the Lonely House, she set out the Third Cup and Saucer and the Third Chair at her table, and called aloud:

"Oh! Little things that came so strangely, help me now, I pray you, send the Ship again to anchor, and *I'll* go away."

Then she drew a long breath and waited. One, two, three minutes passed, then slowly the room began to darken, and then to fill with the cold green light. She ran to the door and opened it, and again she heard the rushing feet, and the cries of the townsfolk as they fled before the storm, leaving only the empty streets behind them.

Breathless she waited until the last footfall had clattered into silence, till the last door slammed shut, and the last bolt shot home, then all alone between the shuttered houses she fled down the rain-splashed streets.

And with a shudder, the people of Hum Drum, behind the safety of their barred and bolted doors, heard through the storm a pair of tiny heels go tap-tap-tapping in a kind of driven haste towards the cobbles of the harbor.

And there the Strange Ship rode at anchor, its tall sides ebon black, its empty decks, and its hollow sails a ghostly white. And the wind shrieked through its rigging like a creature caught in pain.

"Come aboard! No delay, no delay.
Come away! Come away!"

The storm beat upon her, her clothes clung to her as if already she were drowned, but bravely she raised her arms, and struggled across the swaying gangway rimed with the salt of seventy seas, but as her foot lighted on deck, suddenly the storm abated, and the ship slowly, very slowly, put out to sea.

As it did so, terror gripped the Little Loved One, and she ran to the stern of the ship and gazed wildly back at the red roofs of Hum Drum. And she saw the city now in that dazzling clearness which sometimes lightens a sea-windy place after storm, but just as surely spells a wet tomorrow.

Then as slowly but very steadily the Strange Ship passed the cliff on which the old town lay, she raised her tear-stained eyes for one last look at her little Lonely House. And, as she stared with all her heart, suddenly she started, for there, with his hand on the bright brass knocker, stood the Lord Mayor. He had neither coach nor Councilors, nor ermine nor gold chain, but she knew him by his black three cornered hat, and the silver buckles on his shoes.

With a trembling heart the Little Loved One stared towards him, but, as no one answered to his knock, at last she saw him raise his head and gaze upwards at the lattice. Then with a tiny gasp, the Little Loved One saw in the distance the lattice softly open, and a little ivory face, set in a mist of copper-gold, look down at him for a minute, then slowly shake her head, and the lattice close again as the Lord Mayor sadly turned away.

"How strange!" said the Little Loved One, as she shivered on the deck of the Ship, "then my body is still alive," and she turned towards the rigging. But lo! the flag flew white at the mast. At this the Little Loved One shivered again, her teeth began to chatter. Then, as the last of the sunset was swallowed up by the waste of waters, and the roofs of the distant town grew gradually smaller and smaller, she sank down on the deck and wept herself to sleep.

When she awoke it was very dark, and the sea made a loud and angry moan as the Ship cut through the waves. The sky was black without any stars, and her feet were cold as ice. But, as she cowered there, fear could not rob her of all surprise, and to herself she whispered, "I seem to be still alive. Death is different from what I imagined. It seems just a helpless, endless passage through a moaning space, and no more."

Then suddenly, as she raised her head, she heard on the bridge above her a sound that quickened her heart with dread, and flurried her breath with fear, for there in that lonely spot she heard the sound of heavy footsteps pacing the deck.

With a cry of pain she leaped to her feet. "I have suffered enough," she cried. "I will drown my fear in the foam of the waves, for at least I know what they are."

Blind with her dread, she seized the rail to throw herself into the waves. Then, just as she caught this to her, she felt a hand slowly pressing her back to safety. Rubbing the spray from her eyes, in pain she gazed above her, and there, with a lantern held low, she saw a tall Stranger stand.

"What foolishness," he said, "and when we are just in sight of land." And raising his arm he pointed to where a pale light streaked the east.

"What land can it be?" whispered the Little Loved One. "And tell me, who are you?"

"It is the country of tomorrow," said the Stranger, "the land of all beautiful beginnings, and it rests like a dream between heaven and earth."

"But who are you, and how came you here?" the Little Loved One whispered once more. The Stranger smiled into the darkness, then he slowly raised his lantern, and she saw his face, as still, as wonderful as the face of an Eastern prince.

"I seem to have seen you somewhere before," she faltered, "though it must have been in a dream."

"I came most often then," he admitted. "Now, can't you

guess who I am?" But wide eyed she shook her head. "I am your happy ending," he said, "and I should have happened long ago, only you never knew me before, as always I have been disguised as just a passerby."

"But what is your name, and who are you truly?" the Little Loved One whispered again, gazing upwards into his face.

Then just as the sun rose trembling in the distance, the Stranger bent down and slowly kissed her tears.

"I am the Other Person," he said, "and I have loved you from the beginning of the story. Surely you know me now, for to me belong the watching, waiting footsteps, the Third Cup and Saucer—and the Third Lonely Chair."

Barney Loon

THE village street was very steep. And it was lined by glossy chestnut trees as it tumbled in its hurry to reach the sliding loch. By day those trees dropped pools of shadow upon the sunny road. By night they drowned the milk-white cottages and blotted out the moon. Only the large gray houses, ivy grown, that crowned the summit of the hill, escaped their leafy sway, and this because with well-bred ease they held their heads so high above the old brick wall.

Their dark, flat roofs were dated Georgian, and, from their wide-set windows, they kept a watchful eye on all those rusty little thatches toppling with such ill-mannered haste towards the water's brim. In autumn, though their long, steep gardens were damp with blown leaves from the street, and in summer when the ivy on their outer walls was white with village dust, the houses of The Terrace always held themselves aloof, though their iron gates lacked paint, and grass straggled on their pathways.

Now, in the Hardup Village that I'm telling you about, those glossy chestnut trees—so thick with sticky buds in March—were the very special property of that Silent Magician who lives quite close at hand to us (though safely hidden by the rain) in his hand embroidered slippers sewn with stars. And he loved them so well that forever he'd be trimming and retouching them again.

In springtime, when the days grew warm, he would only have to wave his wand above them once or twice, and lo! before you had a moment's notice, they'd be decked around with stiff, trim candles—the cleverest little things that lit themselves at sunset, when the sun fell down the street, and snuffed their lights without a breath the minute that the latest baby bird was bedded for the night.

Then, when the summer weather came and the loch lay still as glass, the magician put the candles out and introduced for coolness' sake those large green flapping fans that wave away the sun so pleasantly when it dallies at midday. And later on (this is the truth I'm telling you) he fancied them a very different way, so when October came with its frosty, smoky dawns, and its yellow torn chrysanthemums, and its bitter smell of burned leaves rising through the pines, the chestnut trees drooped scarlet leaves which stole all color from the old brick wall.

But in the winter weather this Silent Magician had many other things to do, so he forgot the chestnut trees, and left them sorry, stripped, and bare, without a single qualm. And in the cold they shivered and shook, waving their long, lean arms in despair, in a sad and hopeless fury, till the cottage children, lying awake on their warm pillows, would wonder with whom they could be so angry that they shook their arms thus fiercely.

Now this is where my story starts, so gather closely to me, and if you can stop scuffling with your feet upon the floor. . . . I know you hate descriptions, and I'm sorry to be long, but I want you very much to see the vanished village of Hardup, just as Barney and the Beggar used to see it.

Well, in the drowsy summer months when the cottage gardens hummed like hives, and the shadows underneath the leafy chestnuts lay like big sloe-colored saucers in the hot, white dust, the Beggar would come trudging loosely, his thin neck bent beneath his pack, clay on his heels, sand on his toes, and a straw through his buttonhole. Round the corner he would come, glinting his narrow black eyes, smiling that cunning three-cornered smile, twitching his long red nose.

And the cottage children running out to play would watch him wave his skinny fingers above the tiny plants wedged tightly in his pack, and would listen to him calling in his lazy, singsong drawl: "A little spare thyme, a little spare thyme! Two for three farthings! Two for three farthings! A little spare thyme! Come, buy!"

And standing a safe distance off they would mock at him, and hoot, for they knew that he was strange and they could do this, for never on the sunniest day was he known to bring his shadow with him. So standing always out of reach, they would laugh at him and shout, "Beggarman, beggarman, where is your shadow, where have you left it today?"

And over his shoulder the Beggar would answer, glinting his narrow black eyes, "A little spare thyme! A little spare thyme! My shadow is bleaching on Laggart's Brae under a hawthorn tree. I've pinned it down with a pinch of salt. Find it and get your heart's desire with a little spare thyme, a little spare thyme!"

And because they did not understand, and because they were afraid, they pelted him in the hot white dust with little flint-edged stones.

Yet for many sultry mornings, for many hazy noons, for many sun splashed evenings, the Beggar still came limping in his shabby scarecrow clothes and his heavy, earth-filled nails. And, although he made no money in the village that I'm telling you about, he always caused a flutter when he came.

Faces peered behind lace curtains, heads bobbed from garden gates, eyes peeped round laurel bushes, and watched from front-door mats. And this is truth I'm telling you— no one missed the Beggarman's arrival. Even the Blind Man at the corner making string bags in his sleep heard his coming, though he never saw his cunning black eyes glint.

Then the Minister, who used three rooms in his damp and empty manse—that was twice again as drafty as his church, and not so bright—would peer across the privet hedge with his pale, short-sighted eyes. And through a gentle kind of haze he would see the Beggar in the street, and the fresh little plants that bloomed from his pack, and there and then decide to have two.

But always as he hastened down the garden path, fingering his three farthings in the pocket with the hole, he would suddenly remember with a guilty little twinge how much the heathen needed warm and woolly clothing. So (with a tiny sigh which he hardly heard himself) he would drop his penny in the wooden box that begged at his own gate, and turn more slowly up the garden path again, the sun striking hard on his slightly hollow shoulders. . . . And the Beggar would pass down the street with his leather pack as heavy as before.

Then, half along the leafy way, as he trudged through the dust, he'd be sure to meet a bottle-green umbrella and a pair of white kid gloves, and underneath them portly Mrs. Snuthers-Nobbs on her way to pay a call. And always when she saw the Beggar with the thyme, trudging slackly and so loosely through the hot summer day, she would twitch her sandy eyelids, and remember with annoyance a time when she was free from fat and white kid gloves in summer. Then, cherry colored to the brow, she'd go puffing up the street, past that good-for-nothing Tramp, and be extra tart and terse to that afternoon tea party carefully gleaned from the select. . . .

And the Beggar from those shadows, sloe colored in the dust, would go on calling "Spare thyme!" in his lazy, singsong drawl, till the thin-faced Lawyer at the corner, dressed so carefully in gray, with the pleasant smile that children swore was painted to his face, would exclaim: "By Jove! I'll have two!" then falter in his going as he remembered, just in time, that no one dressed so carefully in gray could escape on three farthings with an inch of dignity.

So without another flutter, he'd turn to his trim house

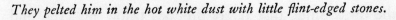

They pelted him in the hot white dust with little flint-edged stones.

with its tidy tussore screens, bowing amiably across the way to poor genteel Miss Snippets of the rectory, who had loved him with no encouragement for fifteen faithful years. . . . And the Beggarman would lose three ha'pence and his temper to the bargain.

Yet farther down the street he'd try his luck once more, and below the stained brick wall that fronts the Doctor's house, he would shift his pack and call again, "Spare thyme!" And the Doctor from his study window would catch a fresh green glimpse and remember certain moments that he thought he had forgotten. He would smile the queer smile that rarely dropped below his eyes, and feel for three farthings, but find he'd only one, and the Beggarman would pass the bend in a scuffle of white dust.

And, this is truth I'm telling you, no one in that village ever bought the Beggarman's spare thyme, till Barney Loon played truant from the school upon the hill.

Now, Barney Loon had never had a father or a mother. He had never had a sister or a brother. And he was such a funny sight that neither you nor I would willingly have claimed him as a cousin, however far removed.

Some people said he must be over eighteen years of age, and others half of that, but no one in the Hardup Village put any money on it, for Barney never altered in the slightest. No one knew where he had come from, though he'd lived there seven years. He just seemed to have happened in the night, and the three maiden ladies who lived in Thimble Cottage often felt annoyed when they saw him playing in the sunshine, smiling his contented smile at nothing in particular.

And yet he never played for very long, for no one ever had more trouble to make ends meet than Barney. He went to school by day for six months in the year and spent his evenings chopping wood, or drawing water from the well for cottagers who lived a thirsty distance from the pump. They never thought of paying him for this, did the people of Hardup, for they were careful souls, and always saved their pennies for the rainy day we're warned about. And as none of them in Hardup had very pleasant outlooks, they simply had to put by every farthing for this heavy private downfall by-and-by.

At harvest in the fields, he toiled from morn till night, sometimes below a blazing sun, but all he ever got on dusty days to slake his fiery little throat was the barley water dribbles in the tin cans when other folk had done. . . . And no one ever paid him in the summer, in case he lost the money on the road. Yet in the broken weather they sometimes let him crawl inside their lofts at night, and in

All he got was the barley water dribbles when other folk had done.

this airy darkness so very near the roof, he slept quite soft and sound among dry, scratchy straw and mice and windfalls of bitter apples.

Now, this is the truth I'm telling you, in all the world Barney had but one good fairy, and she was pretty heavily disguised, even for a fairy in a fairy tale. In fact neither you nor I would ever have discovered her as such unless we'd stood in Barney's boots and she'd proved our sole support. Now this good fairy was the Well-Left Widow Woman, who lived behind the parish church, in the cottage with the fine new slates—so near the church, in fact, that often she was late on Sunday mornings.

But, if any one had chanced to tell her this late moment

was the prettiest and the softest in all her hurried life, she'd have snapped her glasses on her nose, and looked down on them forever. Yet, this is truth I'm telling you, when late each Sunday morning she found the silver plate and the carafe of cold water (that no one dared to drink from) all waiting for her within the silent door, her yellow cheeks would swiftly warm to the color of old rose, and she'd look nearly beautiful for half a fleeting moment.

But no one ever saw her hover slightly tremulous like this, except the gloomy elder, who suffered from cold feet and drafts. *He* for one did *not* approve, and only glanced aloofly at her black and fumbling gloves as she stooped to leave her penny in the polished silver plate.

And though this Widow Woman, who lived behind the church, never wasted words with Barney—she was always pressed for time though she rose a full hour earlier than her neighbors in Hardup—yet she gave him every morning a plate of porridge, and another slightly smaller when the evening came. And on New Year's Day she always added a little golden syrup, for she was much kinder, really, than you would ever have imagined from looking at her face, or her long, bony fingers with their whitened, brittle nails.

But nobody else, that I remember, was very good to

Barney. The other children would not play with him, because they'd heard their mothers say that he was queer and not all there. And they themselves thought poorly of him because he never bore a grudge and because his clothes were mean. Yet it is difficult to say if we'd have cut a better figure in them than poor Barney. There might have been a difference, of course, but yet in them I can't imagine that the friends we're proudest of would, even in a gentle moment, have smiled on us as spruce.

He wore the old blue pantaloons of the Man-next-door-but-one, and his canvas shirt was sewn by thin Miss Snippets in a feverish Dorcas moment, for some little sufferer in the cripple home. Now you couldn't understand the shape of Barney's shirt unless you knew its history as I did, for Miss Snippets at the start had mislaid her *Weekly Weldon,* so she bravely cut it out from memory. As her memories were always far more generous than any hard and fast realities, Barney had to be the gainer at the little sufferer's expense.

His boots—for now we've reached his feet—had come from the Minister, and were useful more as coverings than actual supports, for the soles had known hard other days, and ought certainly to have been pensioned long before they came so far down in the world as Barney. And when he shuffled down the street in them, with that rather constant smile of his, the children would hoot and laugh at him as they hooted at the Beggar.

And though Barney, with a cheerful grin, would always pick their lost balls from the nettles, and still clung round them at their play, they would often hurl ugly names and sticks at him, until he'd have to skip from side to side like a rather clumsy hare to escape them. Yet he never bore a grudge or wore a frown that I remember. Every one in Hardup agreed quite willingly to this that they never saw a frown upon his face, even to the Thimble Cottage ladies, and they could generally see things that other folk had missed.

So this is truth I'm telling you; for the only thing in life he hated was his shock of bright red hair, as he believed it was for this that no one liked him near. They *couldn't* make him see that he was odd, you understand. This was exactly where he showed himself most sadly dense of all.

And sometimes loitering lonely in the cool and shady woods in that air that shimmers softly with little broken sunbeams, the minister's boots tied round his neck, and wet moss squeezing between his crumpled toes, Barney would think those queer little thoughts that were only queerer than other people's because they were short and very clear, and had wider gaps between.

And later, when he'd wearied of wheedling from the gean tree the blackbird, living such a joyous hidden life there, he would wander farther to the birch coppice where sunlight always falls pale green through airy branches. Forever he'd be muttering to himself when he remembered, "It's all my hair. . . . Not me. . . . I can see through a stone dyke farther than the best. . . . It's it . . . or folks 'ud be scuffling for me to clean their yards. . . . For I'm smart. . . . I'm smart. . . . I'm as smart as they make 'em. . . . I can see far more than other folks, though I don't see it the same."

He'd lean his cheek for company against the rough birch bark, till the sunlight straining green through the narrow pointed leaves would make his upturned face as pale as a ghost's, while his fleet thoughts would be scampering through his clouded head like the furry rabbits at his feet. And as he tried to chase those fleeting thoughts, he'd keep muttering to himself, as if in rhyme—

> "For I'm smart,
> I'm smart,
> I'm as smart as they make 'em!"

He beckoned him with a crooked, earth-smudged finger.

But alas! his boasted smartness was just another of those things that no one ever saw the same as Barney. At school he had to sit in class below the Postman's baby girl, aged five. Although he never got beyond his first penny primer, his school days were the hardest of all his days together, for when he tried to read up there before them all, he would sweat so much that the children, poking up bright faces, would notice, amid giggles, that his body often ran with little drops like tears.

And later, when it came to counts, his difficulties grew, for he always seemed to add when the master meant divide—though Barney couldn't see all the difference that it made—and if unhappily he ventured on subtraction, he would find upon the spot that is dedicated to the cane that he'd only multiplied his troubles with this effort.

So when he could, he ran away—and I, for one, don't blame him—although it wasn't always easy, for the master's arm was as long as his sight, and his smooth cane longer still. Yet it happened on one soft spring day that Barney, through the much worn door, slipped quietly off.

Loping heavily down the street with the hum of voices droning behind in the distance, Barney saw for the very last time the Beggarman come trudging, clay on his heels, sand on his toes, and a straw through his buttonhole.

Over his fresh green sprigs he beckoned to Barney, crooking an earth-smudged finger.

"How much, how much do they cost?" asked Barney, skipping steadily nearer, first to the right and then to the left like a rather heavy hare.

"Two for three farthings, two for three farthings!" the Beggarman answered him. "The freshest thyme, the freshest thyme in all the countryside." And then in his lazy, singsong drawl he cried aloud, for the street to hear, although it was almost empty, "My shadow is bleaching on Laggart's Brae, under a hawthorn tree. Find it and get your heart's desire, with a little spare thyme, a little spare thyme!"

"If two sprigs go for three farthings," said Barney, "how much do you take for one?"

"I'll have to do that in my head," said the Beggar, and none too pleased at that. "I've never split them before." And he scratched his head, and shut his eyes, and wrinkled his long red nose. The very next moment his pack swung round, and he felt his chin jerked to the sky, but when he opened his narrow black eyes, Barney was nearing the corner. In the patched blue pantaloons that belonged to the Man-next-door-but-one, he skipped in the dust with glee. "Don't bother to add it up," he cried, "this is where you subtract!" And he scuttled out of sight.

Now, it happened it was Primrose Day that the Beggar
for the last time came to the Hardup Village, and on
Primrose Day at midnight strange things have sometimes
happened in the little silent places of the world, and not
alone to people who are queer like Barney Loon. . . .

That night was a night of wonderful stars that twinkled
and winkled like splinters of ice far up in the watery dark,
when Barney crept under the trees on Laggart's Brae to
look for the Beggarman's shadow, with the sprig of spare
thyme cocked over his ear. Now, Laggart's Brae lies south
to the sun, and its trees bloom always a month too soon,
and are sometimes nipped by the second frost, but the
hawthorns there have the blackest boughs, the sharpest
spikes, the milkiest blossom you ever could wish to
see.

And the night that Barney crept, breathless, among
them under the boughs, they glimmered like ghosts in the
dark, all except one on the brow of the hill, and it stood
naked against the sky, with stars on its spikes, and the
wind whistling through it.

When Barney drew near to this bent, black tree, standing naked against the sky, his heart gave a sudden leap,
and his breath came faster and faster, for under the hawthorn tree, with the wind whistling through it, he saw the
Beggarman's shadow lie, bleached white in the shallow

moonlight. But he felt no fear, just a sudden thrill that warmed him through like wine, for Barney, you know, was a little bit queer, and certainly not all there. In the gusty dark, with a heaving heart, he felt for the sprig of green thyme, and crushed it to pulp in his eager hands and wished for his heart's desire.

Then a wonderful thing slowly happened, for the Beggarman's shadow left to bleach under the hawthorn tree rose silently on to its ghostly feet, and held out its arms to Barney. Its eyes were blind, and its mouth couldn't speak, but its lips smiled palely towards him. With a cry of delight that shocked the silence, he seized its white hands with joy, for though many had laughed at Barney, no one had smiled to him till then.

We do not smile to those who are queer. I don't know why, but we don't. . . . Perhaps because in the nightmare corner each of us hides in our heart, we fear if we share a smile with them we may suddenly have to share the secret that twists thoughts short and clear for good, with clouded gaps between.

And when this wonderful thing happened there in the inky black of the night, the Beggar's shadow jigged up and down, and Barney jigged with him, and the watery air at the top of the Brae gurgled aloud with his laughter.

The Beggar's shadow jigged up and down, and Barney jigged with him.

And round and round the tree they went that stood bent against the sky, with stars on its spikes, and the wind whistling shrilly through it. And those stars that glittered like splinters of ice peered nearer to see the curious dance, and some of them fell as they peered, like arrow heads winged with flame. . . .

Then the Thunder, who lived a watchful life in the far-away hills of Smoak-Blew, heard a rumor of Barney's laughter borne through the rushing air. "I must certainly drown this sound," he said, "or people will think their ears bewitched." And he rumbled so heavily over the valley that the earth below him shook with dread, and the surging loch in the darkness blanched suddenly white as a shroud, then hissed and foamed with fear.

Quick as a flash then the Lightning followed, piercing each keyhole, fencing among the blackened boughs, stabbing the peering stars, so that no one dared gape at Barney whirling in scattered moonbeams with the shadow upon the hill.

And through all that fearsome night, far below them in the village of Hardup the loosened shutters slammed between the windows and the walls, and the lamps at all the corners were snuffed like altar candles, while chimney pots were blown away as light as dandy puffs. . . . And the sudden rain that spurted down upon the blazing embers of each hearth smirched them on the instant into gray and spitting cinders, while the wind that slipped between the cracks in all the fast-barred doors whisked the bedmats from babies' cradles, and blew the salt upon the floor.

Old people crept to bed with eyes as wide as children's, and every one said a prayer that night, and the wicked they said two. In a crazy helter-skelter the storm beat down the street, till the noise of swollen gutters was like a burn in spate. . . .

When morning came at last, and sunshine fell across the drafty street, and the wind had passed behind the sopping woods, the Widow Woman who lives behind the church in the cottage with the fine new slates saw a funny sight come sidling down the rainy road, a figure that she felt she ought to know but didn't.

Its little face was smeared with earth, its naked arms were red with sand, its pantaloons were slimed with moss, and its boots were white with blossom. Beneath her shading, shaking hand the Widow Woman caught her breath, and stared a little harder as it drew a little nearer. . . . Its face was scratched with sharp black thorns that spurted blood in scarlet threads, its hands were cut by jagged flints, its neck was wet with beads of sweat . . . and it smiled a pleasant smile.

Then, as it entered at her gate, the Widow Woman gulped again, and her eyes with fear grew wide as saucers, for in the clear, the morning light, she saw its hair was white as snow. . . . Then she slammed the door and fainted.

And no one ever after that saw Barney Loon again.

Yet since then I've heard it said that after Thunder's been, or Lightning's raked the sky at night, he comes scuffling down the village street in the Minister's old boots —between the glossy chestnut trees that throw by day sloe-colored shadows on the hot, white dust, and by night leave pools like ink to shiver in the wind. And he comes, slowly shuffling among the silent houses of those people who haven't got three farthings left to spare, and when they hear him scuffling in his worn and broken boots, they double bar their doors, and close their shutters, and tell wakeful children if they aren't very careful Barney Loon will catch them and turn them into ghosts.

And why I've told you this is just because we never know what lies in wait for us some Primrose Eve, for when next that Silent Magician, who lives behind the rain, waves his wand for you and me, we may wake to find we've landed in another, very different world to this, where everything is run on lines of topsy-turvy. And our eyes will grow as wide as saucers if we find that everybody adds there where we would multiply, that division is forbidden, and subtraction quite unknown, that the only money coined there is a farthing for good luck, and it's the thing to sweat if you're asked to read a primer.

And if we find ourselves there, we may look rather silly with everybody seeing things different from us both. But if this really happens—and I don't see why it shouldn't—perhaps we mayn't go so far wrong if we do as Barney did, and never bear a grudge though we cannot understand. . . .

Sometimes in moonlight when I look towards Laggart's Brae, and see the trees in blossom there, like ghosts that float in water, and the bent tree at the head of it, black against the sky, with stars on its spikes and the wind whistling through it—my heart gives a daft lilt, and sometimes I think . . . And perhaps in that other world where things are upside down, the folks will all purse their lips and draw themselves away, and look on us as strange and too much there—they may even shut us up in nursing homes—if we bring our shadows with us in the sunshine.

March Cost

March Cost was born Margaret Mackie Morrison in Glasgow, Scotland, and is the eldest member of a family of writers. From an early age she evidenced a keen interest in the arts and between the ages of nine and seventeen she studied drawing, painting, and sculpture at the Glasgow School of Art. Later she studied dramatic art and toured with Sir Frank and Lady Benson's company. After she left the theater, Miss Cost traveled widely. Her journeys have taken her throughout Europe and across the United States.

Miss Cost is known for the superb collection of novels she has written. A Man Named Luke *brought her international fame when it was published in 1932. This was followed by* The Dark

Glass *and* The Dark Star, *which increased her reputation in America and England. After World War II her moving re-creation of the great French actress of the nineteenth century, Rachel, was published as* I, Rachel.

Since then she has written The Bespoken Mile, The Hour Awaits (*a Book-of-the-Month Club selection*), Invitation from Minerva, The Unknown Angel, Her Grace Presents, A Woman of Letters *and* The Interpreter. *In 1963 her first venture into the field of American history,* The Countess, *appeared. This book told the story of Sir Benjamin Thompson, the noted eighteenth-century American-born scientist, who was created Count Rumford, and of his daughter, Sarah, Countess Rumford.*

Among her most recent books are The Year of the Yield *and* After the Festival. Period Pieces, *Miss Cost's first collection of short stories to appear in America, was published by Chilton Book Company in 1966.*